FOOTBALL SHOOTOUT

Bob Temple

illustrated by Sean Tiffany

Librarian Reviewer
Chris Kreie, Media Specialist

Reading Consultant
Mary Evenson, Teacher

www.raintreepublishers.co.uk
Visit our website to find out
more information about
Raintree books.

To order:
☎ Phone 0845 6044371
🖨 Fax +44 (0) 1865 312263
🖳 Email myorders@capstonepub.co.uk

Customers from outside the UK please telephone +44 1865 312262

Raintree is an imprint of Capstone Global Library Limited, a company
incorporated in England and Wales having its registered office at
7 Pilgrim Street, London, EC4V 6LB – Registered company number:
6695582

"Raintree" is a registered trademark of Pearson Education Limited,
under licence to Capstone Global Library Limited

Text © Stone Arch Books, 2008
First published in in the United Kingdom by
Capstone Global Library in 2010
The moral rights of the proprietor have been asserted.

Edited in the UK by Catherine Veitch
Art Director: Heather Kindseth
Graphic Designer: Kay Fraser
Originated by Capstone Global Library
Printed and bound in China by Leo Paper Products Ltd

ISBN 978 1 406213 77 5 (hardback)
14 13 12 11 10
10 9 8 7 6 5 4 3 2 1

ISBN 978 1 406213 98 0 (paperback)
14 13 12 11 10
10 9 8 7 6 5 4 3 2 1

British Library Cataloguing in Publication Data
Temple, Bob.
Football shootout. -- (Sport stories)
813.6-dc22
A full catalogue record for this book is available from the British
Library.

Disclaimer
All the Internet addresses (URLs) given in this book were valid at the
time of going to press. However, due to the dynamic nature of the
Internet, some addresses may have changed, or sites may have changed
or ceased to exist since publication. While the author and publishers
regret any inconvenience this may cause readers, no responsibility for
any such changes can be accepted by either the author or the publishers.

CONTENTS

Chapter 1

SAVING THE DAY

Ben stood along the goal line. His heart was pounding in his chest so loudly that Ben wondered if the other players could actually hear it.

All around him, his teammates screamed for him. "Come on, Ben!" they yelled. "You can do it!"

Parents and friends stood on the sidelines of the pitch. They, too, were yelling and cheering.

Ben danced back and forth on his feet, trying to stay calm. He wiggled his fingers a little to keep them loose.

The penalty kick he was about to face would decide the county championship. Ben always loved playing goalkeeper, but he never realized that the outcome of an entire season might be in his hands.

Ben's team had played a strong game. Joe Fisher, Ben's best friend, had scored the only goal for Ben's team, the Rovers. It was a beautiful, curving shot from just outside the penalty area. But then, Joe always had a great shot.

That's partly how Ben got to be such a great goalie. Practising with Joe and learning how to stop his shots had helped Ben to improve his game.

Joe's goal had given the Rovers a 1–0 lead early in the second half. With about ten minutes left in the game, the Wanderers had tied the score.

The Wanderers had a corner kick, and the player dropped the ball perfectly in front of the net. One of the Rovers' defenders missed a chance to clear it, and a Wanderers player made a direct shot at the goal.

Ben made a dive and stopped it, but the rebound went right to another player, who put it in the goal. Ben felt horrible, but the goal wasn't really his fault.

The rest of the game was close, but neither team had a great chance to score.

When the game ended in a draw, 1–1, it meant that penalties would decide the winner.

Each team selected five players to take penalty kicks against the other team's goalkeeper. Whichever team scored the most goals would win the game.

Ben stopped the first two shots he faced, but the next two shots flew past him. The first two Rovers missed their shots, but the last three players all scored. Joe took the final shot and blasted it into the upper-right corner of the goal.

Now the Rovers were leading 3–2, and the Wanderers had only one shot remaining. If Ben stopped it, the Rovers were county champions. If not, each team would have another shot.

The referee approached Ben and reminded him of the rules. "Remember, you can't move forward until the ball is kicked," he said. Ben nodded.

Then, the ref turned to the last shooter. "You can go on my whistle," he said. The boy nodded.

The Wanderers player was one of their best forwards. He was the boy who had scored their only goal of the game. He had tried two attempts against Ben earlier in the game. Both times, he had tried to bend the ball towards the right side of the net. Would he do it again?

Ben bent his knees. He put his hands up in the way his coach had taught him. All around him, people screamed. The noise didn't bother Ben. In fact, he was so focused on the play that he barely noticed.

The player placed the ball on the penalty spot. He backed away from it, lining up his shot.

Ben felt a bead of sweat roll down his cheek. The other boy eyed the net.

As the two boys moved into place, the crowd fell silent. Finally, the referee's whistle broke the silence.

It was time.

Both players gathered themselves for a moment.

As the Wanderers player prepared to take his kick, Ben felt a surge of confidence rise up in his chest. This was it. The county title was on the line. He was ready.

The Wanderers player ran towards the ball. Ben had only an instant to work out which way he would shoot the ball.

Would he go right again, as he had before?

Ben started to lean that way. Then, as the boy's leg pulled back to take the shot, Ben could see what was happening. It looked like the boy was going to play the ball with the outside of his foot, pushing it toward Ben's left.

Ben timed his dive to the moment the boy made contact with the ball. Just as Ben expected, the boy pushed the ball towards Ben's left. Ben took a quick step that way and made a low dive, directly towards the spot the ball was going.

It was a near-perfect shot. It was low and hard, heading for just inside the left goalpost.

But Ben's dive was right out of the goalkeeping textbook. His gloved left hand met the ball near the corner, pushing it out past the post.

No goal!

The Rovers players leapt into the air and screamed. They rushed to the goal as Ben got back on his feet.

Ben had made the save!

All the players piled on him to celebrate their first county championship.

Chapter 2

ANOTHER PLAYER?

The football season ended. Winter turned to spring, and spring turned to summer. Ben and Joe played hockey in the winter. Ben played tennis in the summer, and Joe played cricket. But for both boys, these other sports were just to keep in shape. Football was their favourite sport.

When it was nearly autumn and the weather was getting cooler, the boys began to start thinking even more about football.

Autumn term meant trials and the start of another season.

It would be a chance for the boys to defend their county championship with the Rovers.

Ben and Joe practised as much as they could. They would go to the field after school, and Joe would practise shooting against Ben.

Ben worked on his dives, his footwork, and other skills.

One day, Ben arrived at school a little late. He strolled into his first lesson just before the bell rang.

He took his seat in the row nearest the door. As always, he glanced across the room at Joe and gave him a nod.

Joe had a strange look on his face. He seemed to want to tell Ben something. Ben furrowed his brow, then gave Joe a look that said, "What's up?" Joe tried to whisper something, but the teacher interrupted.

"Boys?" the teacher said. "Is there a problem?"

"Ah, no," Joe said. "Sorry."

For the rest of the period, the boys concentrated on their work.

When the bell rang to end the class, Ben waited for Joe by the door.

"What is it?" Ben asked. "What's going on?"

Joe turned to face his friend. "There's a new boy," Joe said.

"What? A new boy in school?" Ben replied.

"Yeah," Joe said. "And apparently he's a really good football player."

Ben thought about the comment for a minute. He wasn't sure what to say.

"Somebody said he was from Scotland, which has some really good football teams," Joe said.

Ben's face lit up. "Cool!" he said. "If he's really good, we'll win county again this year for sure!"

Joe didn't seem as happy. "Ben," he said. "You don't understand."

Ben stopped and looked back at Joe. He could tell something was wrong. Then, Ben worked it out. The new boy must be a forward.

Since Joe was a forward, too, he was probably worried about his playing time, Ben thought.

"Look, Joe," Ben said. "If he's a forward, there's no way he's as good as you are."

Joe shook his head. "No, Ben," he said. "That's not it."

"Then what?" Ben asked. "What can be so bad about a new boy who can play football?"

"Ben," Joe said. "The new boy is a goalkeeper."

Chapter 3

MEET THE NEW BOY

Ben shrugged.

"So what?" he said. "I'm not worried. After all, I helped us win the county championship last year. It's not like the coach is going to replace me just because some new boy is on the scene."

Joe nodded. "Yeah, you're right," he said.

Ben wasn't nearly as confident as he was letting on.

Deep down, he was worried about the new boy.

All day long, other boys from his team were talking about the new boy.

"I heard he's six feet tall," one boy said.

"I heard he can kick the ball into the other team's goal," another said.

Ben knew the stories were ridiculous, but they were starting to bother him.

Finally, after lunch, Ben got to meet the new boy.

Ben sat down in his maths lesson.

Just before the bell rang, the new boy walked into the room. He talked quietly with the teacher for a moment. Then he took a seat near the front of the room.

Ben was sitting two rows back.

The new boy was tall, yes, but he wasn't that tall. He seemed like he was probably a pretty good athlete, though.

When maths class ended, Ben decided he should introduce himself. Ben approached the boy from behind and tapped him on the shoulder.

"Hey, I'm Ben," Ben said. "I hear you play football."

"Too right," the boy said. "I'm James. I hear you lot are good."

Ben chuckled. "Well, we won the county title last year," he said. "So yeah, we're pretty good."

James shrugged his shoulders and rolled his eyes. "We won the Scottish league," James said. "And we take football very seriously in Scotland."

Ben tried not to let the boy's comment get to him. "I think you might be surprised at how well we can play," he said. He let out a little laugh to try to ease any tension.

"I guess I'll find out at trials," James said. "We'll see if any of you boys can score against me."

Ben paused. "Oh, so you're a goalie?" he said, pretending to act surprised. James nodded. Ben paused for a moment, then said, "Me too."

James looked him up and down. "Hmm," he said. "So I guess it's you against me at trials. Well, it's nice to know who the competition is."

"Yeah, it is," Ben replied. Now he was trying to act tough. But deep down, the other guy's confidence was getting to him.

Chapter 4

TRIALS

Ben used the few weeks remaining before trials to practise harder than he ever had before. It was early autumn and the days were getting shorter. Ben convinced Joe to go out to the football pitches behind school to practise with him.

They practised close-in shots and long, curving shots. They practised defending against corner kicks. They practised penalty kicks and dribbling.

Ben practised his goal kicks, too. He wanted to make sure he was ready.

Finally, on the first day of trials, Coach Davis pulled Ben aside.

"Hey, Ben," the coach said. "How are you feeling about trials?"

"I'm ready," Ben said. "No worries."

Coach Davis smiled. "I'm sure you've met the new boy," he said. "James looks like a good player. But I don't want you to worry."

Ben felt a huge sense of relief. The coach was telling him the job was his. But before Ben could relax too much, Coach Davis gave him a surprise. "I'm going to make sure the competition is as fair as possible," the coach said. "May the best player win."

The coach patted Ben on the back and trotted away.

"What?" Ben thought to himself. "Competition?"

Then Ben knew the game was on. He would have to play at his best in order to keep his job as the Rovers' goalkeeper.

It didn't take long for the differences between Ben and James to become clear during trials.

As they worked on various drills, Ben was clearly better at many of the technical parts of the game.

He made good decisions on when to come out of the goal to challenge a player or to pick up a loose ball. He always seemed to be in the right place at the right time.

When shots were fired at him, Ben made solid saves and controlled the rebounds.

James was a little wilder in the goal. He took unnecessary chances, coming out of the net to challenge a player when it would have been smarter to stay back. He often found himself out of place.

But James was a better athlete than Ben. So he often covered for his own mistakes by making spectacular diving saves.

James could kick the ball much further than Ben, but Ben's kicks were more on target to a teammate.

On the second-to-last day of trials, Coach Davis broke the Rovers into two teams for a practice match.

The teams were pretty evenly matched. Ben was in one goal, James was in the other. Joe was on Ben's team.

Before the practice match, Joe ran up to Ben. "Don't worry, mate," he said. "I'll score against him and then you'll have the goalie job."

At first, the pratice match was going just as the drills had gone. Ben was always in the right place.

When any shots were taken at him, Ben was ready, so the saves were pretty easy to make.

James was running all over the field. At one point, he charged at a forward who had the ball in the corner. That left the whole goal wide open, so the forward lobbed a pass towards Joe.

Joe met the pass in the penalty area. He controlled the ball with his left foot, then blasted it with his right towards the open net. But James's speed allowed him to get back to the net. He lunged across to his right and deflected Joe's shot towards the right post.

Another forward pulled the rebound in on the right side of the net.

Again James charged, and the forward put the ball in front of him.

This time Joe tried to redirect the ball towards the left post. He didn't aim it perfectly, and James flung himself on top of the loose ball.

Ben's heart sank. He knew that if the same play had happened to him, neither of those shots would have been taken.

He would have stopped the first pass, and the play would have been over. But James's wild style allowed him to make two spectacular-looking saves. Even Coach Davis was clapping and yelling.

Neither team scored in the practice match. Afterwards, Coach Davis called Ben over to the sideline. "Ben," he said. "I have an idea."

Idea? Ben wasn't sure what to say.

Then the coach continued: "Have you ever thought about playing in another position?"

Chapter 5

NEW POSITION?

Ben decided to be honest with his coach.

"Um, no, Coach," he said. "I've always wanted to be a goalkeeper."

Coach Davis put his arm around Ben's shoulder.

"Well, you have such great footwork, and you're always in the right place at the right time," Coach Davis said. "I think you will make a great sweeper."

The sweeper plays right in front of the goalie. He is often the goalie's most trusted teammate.

The sweeper helps protect the goalkeeper and clears away loose balls in front of the net.

It was a very important position, Ben knew. And since Matt Singh, the boy who played it last season, had moved, the position was open.

Still, Ben wasn't interested in it. "I'd rather play goalie," he said.

"I know," Coach Davis said. "But I think I'm going to go with James in goal."

Ben was shocked.

It had been a long time since he'd cried about anything to do with sport, but he felt like it now.

"You'll be the backup goalie," Coach Davis continued. "And you'll still play all the time, because you'll be the sweeper."

Ben managed to mutter something that sounded like "Okay," but he was still fighting back tears.

As the players left the pitch, he ran off ahead of the group.

He changed clothes quickly and got on his bike for the short ride home.

One more day of trials remained, but Ben already knew where he stood.

On the final day of trials, he didn't even bring his goalkeeper gloves to the field. He practised the entire time with the defenders.

During a break, Joe ran up to Ben.

"What on earth are you doing?" Joe asked. "Why aren't you fighting for the goalie spot?"

"Coach Davis told me yesterday," Ben said. He couldn't bear to look at his friend. He kept his eyes fixed on the ground. "I'm going to be the sweeper."

"That stinks," Joe said. "At least you'll be on the field all the time with me."

Ben smiled a little. Just then, James ran over for a drink of water. He walked right up to the boys. Ben cringed as he prepared for James to gloat.

"Hey, Ben," James said. "You're a good goalie. I'm sorry trials didn't turn out the way you wanted."

Ben was sure James didn't mean what he said. "Yeah," Ben said. "Whatever."

"It was a good competition," James said. He held out his hand to Ben. "No hard feelings?"

Ben shook James's hand for a quick second. "No hard feelings," he forced out. James trotted away.

"What's up with that boy?" Ben said to Joe. "He's Mr Cool one minute, then pretends to be nice the next."

Joe was sure he knew what was going on.

"He's just trying to butter you up," Joe said, "because he knows that all season you'll be protecting him."

Chapter 6

LET THE GAMES BEGIN

After just a few weeks of practice, the Rovers were ready to begin their season.

They had a long fixture list. There were twenty-four league games, plus the county tournament.

Before the Rovers' first game of the season, Coach Davis gathered the players around for a pep talk.

"Well, boys, we're ready for another great season," he began. "Last year, we won the county tournament. I know some things are different this year, but I think we can do it again. And we have a new opportunity this year. Whoever wins the county title this year will be invited to play in a national tournament!"

Now the players were fired up. They couldn't wait to get on the pitch.

When the game began, Ben felt strange. Playing as sweeper meant moving around the field a lot and doing things that he wasn't used to doing.

Still, he handled the position well, so James didn't have much work at the net.

The Rovers controlled play for most of the game.

Joe scored a goal late in the first half to give the team a 1–0 lead against their opponents, the Stripes.

Early in the second half, the Stripes became more aggressive. They kept putting pressure on the Rovers' goal. Ben and the rest of the defenders were kept busy clearing the ball away.

Midway through the half, the Stripes pushed the ball down into the left corner of the pitch. James charged out of the net to challenge the forward. That left the net empty.

"James!" Ben yelled. "Get back in the goal!"

It was too late.

A Stripes player hit the ball into the middle of the pitch.

Ben couldn't get to it, and the Stripes's centre forward pounded the ball into the open net. James dived, but couldn't reach the shot.

As James dug the ball out of the goal, Ben walked over to him.

"James, don't charge into the corners," he said, as nicely as possible. "You have to stay in the net. Let your defense handle the corners."

"Maybe you should have cleared that ball away," James snapped back. "You made me look bad."

Ben turned and trotted back onto the pitch. Minutes later, the Stripes had another chance from the corner. James charged again, and again the ball was kicked over his head.

This time, Ben slid in front of the forward and knocked the ball away.

When the ball was cleared to the other end of the pitch, Ben turned back towards James.

"See?" Ben said. "You have to stay in the goal. That time, I saved you!"

Chapter 7

A LITTLE HELP

The Stripes and the Rovers ended the game in a 1–1 tie.

The rest of the Rovers' season was a lot like that first game.

James made some great saves, but his poor play cost his team several goals.

The Rovers were scoring as many goals as they had the year before, but they were giving up a lot more.

Joe led the team with sixteen goals, but instead of winning games 2–1 or 1–0, the Rovers were losing 3–2 or tying 2–2.

After that first game, when James didn't seem to like Ben's advice, Ben stopped giving it. He did his best job as sweeper, trying to protect James. But he didn't offer James any help in how to play goalkeeper.

At this rate, the Rovers were not going to make the county tournament.

So far, their season record of ten wins, six losses, and four ties put them in fourth place.

They would have to win at least three more league games and the county tournament in order to have a chance at going to the national tournament.

It seemed very unlikely.

It took the whole season, but finally Coach Davis saw that James's risky play was hurting the team.

After the last game of the regular season, he took James aside for a private chat. Ben couldn't hear what they were saying.

When the chat was over, Coach Davis called to Ben.

Ben ran up to him.

"Ben, I think we need to make a change," Coach Davis said. "I'd like to put you back in goal for the rest of the league games."

Ben wasn't sure what to say. He glanced across the field and saw James.

The tall boy was walking away slowly, his head held low.

"Are you sure?" Ben said. "James's been playing there all year."

"It's not working out," Coach Davis said. "If we want to go to nationals, we need you in goal."

It was a huge compliment, and Ben knew it.

Still, he felt uneasy. "Um, thanks, Coach," he finally said.

As the coach walked away, Joe approached. "I heard the great news!" he yelled. "That's fantastic!"

"Yeah, great," Ben mumbled. "So why don't I feel better?"

That night at home, Ben pulled out his goalkeeper gloves. He tried them on. This time, they felt a little strange.

Ben stared at the gloves, and things suddenly became clear.

That night, Ben phoned Joe and asked if he could meet at the football pitch.

"Trust me," Ben told his friend. "I have an idea."

Chapter 8

HELPING OUT

Ben walked over to James's house. He rang the doorbell and waited.

He wasn't sure how James would react to him coming over. After all, they weren't exactly friends.

James came to the door. When he saw Ben, he paused for a moment. Then he opened the door and stepped out.

"So, did you come over to gloat?" James said.

"Not exactly," Ben said. "I have an idea."

James looked confused.

Ben didn't worry about what he was about to say.

He decided direct honesty was the only way.

"Look, you make better saves than I do," Ben said. "But you're not a better goalkeeper than me."

"So you did come over to gloat," James shot back.

"Just listen," Ben replied. "If we put our skills together, we'd have an amazing goalkeeper. So that's what we need to do."

"Huh?" James said. "What are you saying? Are you crazy?"

"We need to combine our skills into one goalie," Ben said. "I'll never be able to make some of the amazing saves you make, because you're a better athlete than I'll ever be. But you can learn how to play goalkeeper as well as I do."

It was all becoming clear to James. "So, you're going to help me with the basics?" he said.

"Exactly," Ben said.

* * *

Throughout that weekend, Ben and Joe drilled James on the basics.

They worked on helping James decide when to charge and when to stay in the goal. They even worked out a series of signals that Ben could give to James to help him hold his place.

It wasn't easy, but James was starting to get it.

* * *

At the next practice, Ben and James approached Coach Davis together.

They presented their idea, and told the coach what they had already done.

Coach Davis seemed pleased.

"I'm not sure if this will work," he said. "But I'm proud of you boys for working together to solve this problem. Let's do it!"

Chapter 9

PLAN IN ACTION

It wasn't always smooth, but the plan worked.

Ben shouted "Goal!" whenever James needed to stay put, and "Now!" when he needed to charge.

After a few games, Ben didn't need to make the calls anymore.

James was working it out on his own.

James kept making spectacular saves.

This time the saves were keeping the Rovers ahead instead of covering up James's own bad decisions. It made playing goalkeeper much easier.

The Rovers easily advanced through the league games and the first two rounds of the county tournament.

In the county championship, they again faced the Wanderers, just as they had the year before. This was it, their chance to go to nationals for the first time ever.

The Wanderers were a great team, and they had a powerful offence. That was clear in the first half, when the Wanderers pressured the Rovers' goal.

Ben and the rest of the defence kept the ball away from the goal for most of the half.

James made a few saves, too, and did a great job of playing the position.

Early in the second half, Ben intercepted a pass at the top of the penalty area.

Looking ahead, he heard Joe yell "Send it!" as he took off down the sideline. Ben booted the ball high down the field, ahead of Joe.

With his speed, Joe beat the defence and controlled the pass.

He closed on the Wanderers goal and blasted a heavy shot towards the far upper corner.

As the ball hit the net, Ben and the rest of the Rovers yelled.

They were ahead!

Now they only needed to protect their lead. Against the Wanderers, it wasn't going to be easy.

Throughout the rest of the half, the Wanderers put pressure on the goal. Like many teams, they tried to advance the ball to the corners, then cross it into the middle of the pitch.

James never budged at those times. He was able to intercept several crosses as a result.

In the final minute, the Wanderers made one last rush up the pitch. They moved the ball into the corner, and a Rovers defender rushed to challenge.

Ben moved to cover a player. But with the game on the line, the Wanderers brought more players into the area.

The Rovers defenders couldn't cover them all.

The Wanderers player kicked the ball towards the front of the goal.

James froze. Ben could tell he was trying to decide if he should run out to try and play it or if he should stay in the goal.

James stayed put. He saw the ball going towards an unguarded player near the penalty spot.

James prepared for the shot. He crouched low and kept his hands ready.

When the ball bounced off the player's foot, James was ahead of it.

His sprawling dive met the ball perfectly. And, instead of knocking it away, James

caught it. He clutched it tightly as the full-time whistle went.

The Rovers were champions again!

Joe and Ben rushed to their goalie. James still held the ball to his chest.

"You did it!" Ben yelled. "You did it!"

James looked him in the eye. "No, we did it," James said.

About the Author

Bob Temple has written more than thirty books for children. Over the years, he has coached more than twenty kids' football, basketball, and baseball teams. He also loves visiting classrooms to talk about his writing.

About the Illustrator

When Sean Tiffany was growing up, he lived on a small island. Every day, he had to take a boat to get to school. When Sean isn't working on his art, he works on a multimedia project called "OilCan Drive", which combines music and art. He has a pet cactus named Jim.

Glossary

dribble take the ball forward past other players with slight touches of the feet

drill a set work routine

forward attacking player in football. Also called a striker.

penalty kick in football, an extra shot awarded against a team that has committed an offence

penalty spot place on the pitch from which a player makes a penalty kick

rebound to bounce the ball back into play

sweeper player whose job it is to protect the goalkeeper and clear away loose balls in front of the net

trial test to see if someone is capable of playing a sport

More About Football Positions

A football team is made up of eleven players: forwards, midfielders, defenders, and a goalkeeper.

The forwards are responsible for most of the team's scoring. Since they play in front of the rest of the team, they can take the most shots.

Midfielders play directly behind the forwards. They help with ball control and passing.

The defenders are next in line. They keep the other team's players from scoring.

Finally, the goalkeeper prevents shots from crossing the goal line.

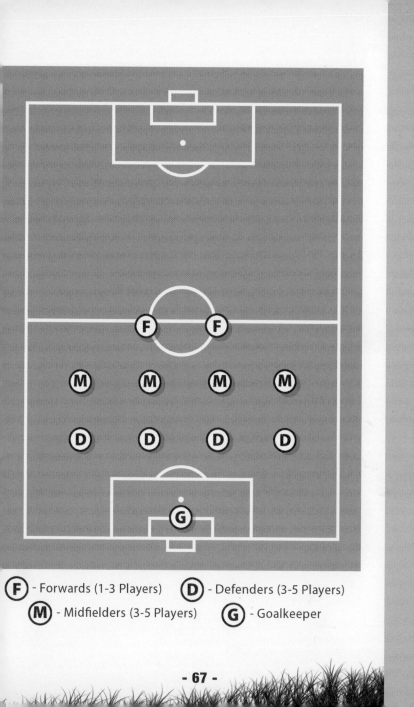

F - Forwards (1-3 Players)   **D** - Defenders (3-5 Players)

M - Midfielders (3-5 Players)   **G** - Goalkeeper

Discussion Questions

1. Why do you think James acted the way he did when he first arrived at his new school?

2. Ben could have made James look bad by letting the other teams take some good shots against him. Instead, Ben tried his best to protect James. Why?

3. Coach Davis offered Ben a chance to be the goalkeeper again. Why do you think Ben felt strange about that?

Writing Prompts

1. At the beginning of the book, Ben faced a situation in which the outcome of the game depended on him. Write about a time when there was a lot of pressure on you, and how you handled it.

2. Have you ever been replaced by someone else, like Ben was? Write about how that felt.

3. At the end of the book, Ben did something to help out James. Write about a time when you helped someone achieve something great.

Hannah and Max have the run of Snowstream, a cool winter resort. But a new boy, Zach, starts a boys-only snowboard cross team. What will Max do when he's forced to choose between Hannah and snowboarding?

Matt's chances of making the racing team are threatened when Alex moves into town. Alex is a cheat, and as mean as they come out on the racetrack. Matt insists on riding by the rules. Unless somebody stops Alex cheating, Matt wont make the team...

Find out more

Books

Football Mad, John Goodwin, Alan MacDonald, Helena Pielichaty (Oxford University Press, 2008)

Sports Files: Wayne Rooney, John Townsend (Raintree, 2009)

Football Skills, Clive Gifford (Kingfisher Books, 2005)

Football Detective: Foul Play, Tom Palmer (Puffin, 2008)

Websites

www.thefa.com
Find out everything you need to know about the FA and English football.

www.bbc.net.uk/sportacademy
Pick up football tips and tricks. Download a football mask.